PRINCESS BUN BUN

Richard Scrimger • Illustrated by Gillian Johnson

Tundra Books

Published in Canada by Tundra Books,
481 University Avenue, Toronto, Ontario M5G 2E9

Published in the United States by Tundra Books of Northern New York,
P.O. Box 1030, Plattsburgh, New York 12901

Library of Congress Control Number: 2001095518

National Library of Canada Cataloguing in Publication Data

Scrimger, Richard, 1957-
   Princess Bun Bun

ISBN 0-88776-543-2

I. Johnson, Gillian.   II. Title.

PS8587.C745P75 2002   jC813'.54   C2001-902945-4
PZ7.S43617Pr 2002

We acknowledge the support of the Canada Council for the Arts and the Ontario
Arts Council for our publishing program.

We acknowledge the financial support of the Government of Canada through the
Book Publishing Industry Development Program for our publishing activities.

Design: K.T. Njo

Printed in Hong Kong, China

1 2 3 4 5 6   07 06 05 04 03 02

For my brother – my kids' Uncle Dave

R.S.

———

For Lizzy

G.J.

Winifred was going to visit Uncle Dave in his new castle. That's what he called it. "Is it a real castle?" Winifred asked her mother.

"It's a condominium," said Mommy. "It's called Castle Apartments."

"I wonder if there'll be a moat, and a spiky door," Winifred said to her brother, Eugene.

"I wonder if there'll be juice in the fridge," he said.

"I hope there's a guard, with a sword."

"I hope there's a TV," said Eugene.

Castle Towers didn't have a moat or a
spiky door. There was a guard, but he didn't
have a sword. He had a phone. He phoned
Uncle Dave, and then let them in.

    "Will there be a princess in this castle?" asked Winifred.

    Daddy laughed. Mommy poked him in the ribs. "I don't think so," she said.

    Bun Bun tottered through the lobby. Her real name was Brenda, but no
one called her that.

    "Look, Winifred!" cried Mommy. "Bun Bun is walking! Isn't that wonderful!"

    "She was walking last week," Winifred told the guard.

"I will push the button to call the elevator!" cried Winifred.

"No, I will!" cried Eugene.

They both rushed forward.

One elevator made a loud clunk. The doors opened. Bun Bun took another step and another. And another. She walked right into the elevator.

"Oh, no!" cried Daddy.
Winifred hurried in after Bun Bun. The doors closed.
"Oh, no," said Winifred.

The elevator started to
go up. "Now see what
you've done, Bun Bun!"
said Winifred. She wondered
what to do. She could push
a button, but which one?

"This is all your fault,
Bun Bun!" Winifred said.
"If you didn't know how
to walk, this never would
have happened!"

Bun Bun started to cry.
Winifred picked her up.
"There there," she said.
Just like Mommy.

Mommy. Winifred thought
of Mommy, waiting below.

The elevator stopped. *Were they at the top of the tower?* The doors opened, and –
"Oh, no! A monster!"
Of course there would be a monster in the castle! A monster, with a long nose and sharp teeth and a tongue like a wet towel.
Winifred put Bun Bun down and pressed the nearest button.
Was it the right one?
The doors shut. **Whew!**
That was close.
The elevator went up and up and . . . stopped again.

The doors opened and – there was
a witch! Gray hair, and a broom.
And a black cat!
"Hello, dearie," said the witch.
Winifred stood on tiptoe to
press the button. The witch
looked puzzled, but didn't get on.
The doors shut. Bun Bun was
sitting on the floor, taking off
her shoes.
"Oh, Bun Bun, you are so
messy!" said Winifred. Just
like Mommy.
Mommy! Winifred felt tears
prickling behind her eyelids.
She brushed them away.

Next time the doors opened,
Winifred stared up at a
beautiful lady.

    "Are you a princess?"
asked Winifred.

     "Sometimes," said the
beautiful lady. "Is this elevator
going up or down?"

      "Up." Winifred frowned.
*How could you be a
sometime princess?*

       "Sometimes I'm a
girl-next-door," said
the beautiful lady,
as the doors closed.

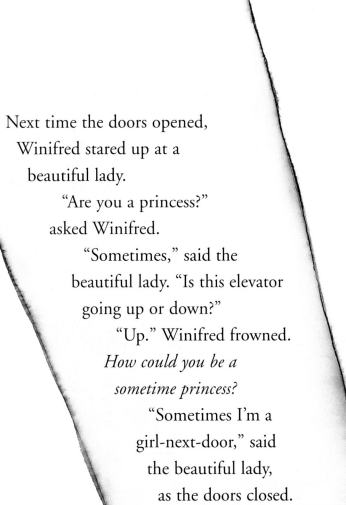

Up and up. The elevator stopped with a **thud**.
Who would be waiting this time? A knight in armor?
A dragon? The doors opened on . . . nothing.

Winifred and Bun Bun peered out.

"Wait! Hold the elevator!" A shadowy figure
raced towards them. It was not a knight in armor,
or a dragon. It was Uncle Dave.

"Hi, kids!" he said. "Where's your mom and dad?"

"Downstairs," said Winifred. "Oh, Uncle Dave, the elevator went up all by itself."

"Well, it can't go up anymore," said Uncle Dave. "This is the top floor."

He picked up Bun Bun and got on the elevator. They went down without stopping once.

Mommy and Daddy were very happy
to see Winifred and Bun Bun again.
They hugged them and hugged them.
"We were so worried!" they said.

"Why?" said Winifred. "We were fine.
I stopped the monster and the witch from
getting on the elevator with us."

"What monster?" asked Uncle Dave.

"What witch?" asked Daddy.

"He really does live in a castle, you know, Eugene," said Winifred. "There's even a princess. I saw her."

"Did you see a TV?" asked Eugene.

"A princess?" Uncle Dave opened the bag he was carrying, and went down on one knee. "The only princesses in my castle are Princess Winifred and Princess Bun Bun."

Winifred wrinkled her nose.

Princess Bun Bun didn't say anything.